Going Green!

Franzeska G. Ewart

illustrated by Georgie Birkett

SCHOLASTIC

To Julia Donaldson, with thanks

Scholastic Children's Books,
Commonwealth House, 1–19 New Oxford Street,
London, WC1A 1NU, UK
a division of Scholastic Ltd
London ~ New York ~ Toronto ~ Sydney ~ Auckland
Mexico City ~ New Delhi ~ Hong Kong

First published by Scholastic Ltd, 2003

Text copyright © Franzeska G. Ewart, 2003
Illustrations copyright © Georgie Birkett, 2003

ISBN 0 439 97698 7

Printed and bound by Nørhaven Paperback A/S, Denmark

2 4 6 8 10 9 7 5 3 1

Going Green!

Wallace and Majid

*Look out for more stories
about this terrible twosome!*

Bugging Miss Bannigan

Chapter One

It was a sunny spring morning at Grimstone Primary, and Wallace Meek and Wajid Haq were enjoying their mid-morning snacks.

As usual they were sitting snugly in S.P.E.W., the Special Place by the Wheeliebins; and, as usual, the air was filled with its many and varied smells. This morning the atmosphere was particularly fishy, with just a hint of cauliflower cheese. There was also, if you really concentrated, the subtle undertone of yesterday's steamed pudding.

Wallace took the foil wrapper off an oatcake, broke it in half, and handed it to Wajid. Wajid thanked him and gave him a large slab of pistachio-flavoured burfee in return. They chewed happily.

"Well, Wajid," said Wallace, licking his lips, "Miss Bannigan has done it again! This Environmental Awareness project of hers is just what Grimstone Primary needs."

Wajid nodded enthusiastically. "As she says – you're never too young to care for the

Earth. And the school looks a lot better since we got our anti-litter campaign going."

He sniffed the air. "Still room for improvement though. Doesn't half smell round here!"

"Sure," said Wallace. "But it's what keeps certain people out of our hair, if you get my drift..." He tapped the side of his nose and winked at Wajid.

Wajid laughed and nodded. "Sure, Wallace. If it was a toss-up between Melanie and Jasbir and the smell of last week's smoked haddock, I know what I'd choose!"

And he sat back and breathed in the air happily. Then he turned to Wallace, eyes bright. "The best bit of all is that we might get chosen to be on *Let's Go GREEN!* It's my favourite television programme!"

"Mine too," agreed Wallace. "It's so zippy, isn't it – the way they rush around the country, finding all sorts of ways to improve the environment!"

He gave a thumbs-up sign. "I love it when they say 'Let's go what?'"

Wajid bounced up and down with excitement. "Oh yes!" he said. "And then everyone screams, 'Let's go GREEN!'"

He bit his lip. "Do you think we've really got a chance of being picked?"

Wallace considered this. "Grimstone's up against all the schools in the area," he said doubtfully. "It'll be tough."

"Supposing – just supposing, we did," Wajid went on, his voice quivering with emotion, "then someone in Year Five would get to be the Kid Presenter. And that someone could be me! Now that would be a dream come true!"

"Really?" said Wallace in surprise. "You'd like to be a television presenter?"

"More than anything else in the whole wide world, Wallace," Wajid told him. "Any kind of presenter – but most of all, I'd love to read the news or the weather." And he hugged his knees tight to stop them shaking.

The bell rang and as they both jumped up, Wajid plugged in the Radio Aid that connected to his hearing aids. Miss Bannigan wore a transmitter, so that Wajid could always hear what she was telling the class. Suddenly he stopped, adjusted the volume, and hissed at Wallace.

"Hey! Hang on a minute – bit of news coming through!" And he handed Wallace the right hearing aid. They walked to their class line as slowly as they dared, listening eagerly to the voice coming from the staffroom. Miss Bannigan sounded more breathless and excited than usual. It was clear she was talking to some very special people.

"They've arrived!" breathed Wallace.

"Sean Sting and Shazia Khan, the presenters of *Let's Go GREEN!*" Wajid gasped. "We're going to see them – in the flesh!"

And, in a daze of excitement, they joined the line.

Chapter Two

Melanie and Jasbir were last in line when Wallace and Wajid got there. They had been deep in whispered conversation, but when they saw the boys approach Jasbir nudged Melanie and they stopped and stood to attention facing the door.

Just as Mr Parsons the Year Six teacher emerged, Jasbir turned round. "Melanie and me have got an act that'll knock the television people dead," she told them, jabbing her finger at them as she spoke.

"So, if you two were thinking up some half-baked scheme of your own, just forget it!" Melanie put in.

"Leave it to those of us with star quality, OK?" concluded Jasbir firmly.

"Year Five, silence in line!" roared Mr Parsons. Melanie and Jasbir both closed their lips and placed a forefinger on top. Then they turned back to Wallace and Wajid and glared at them accusingly.

"Never said a flipping word," whispered Wallace indignantly to Wajid, as they filed in.

"Never get a word in edgeways with those two," agreed Wajid, and they lowered their heads and marched exactly in step past the teacher, who glared down at them suspiciously and muttered vaguely, "Just watch it..."

"Don't know how he does it, Wajid,"
Wallace said when they were safely in the
classroom. "He seems to know what we're
thinking just from the backs of our necks.
Clever though – you've got to hand it to him."

"Probably something they teach them at
College," Wajid observed. Then, glancing
round to make sure Mr Parsons was well out
of the way, he picked up the blackboard
pointer and stood at the board.

"Good afternoon, viewers," he announced
to the class. "This
is Wajid Haq,
with all the
weather
that *is*
weather!"

assessing
conclusion
necessary
opportunity

"Ignore him," Jasbir muttered darkly from the back.

"And it's a grim forecast for this afternoon, I'm afraid," Wajid went on, undaunted. He swept the pointer over the surface of the blackboard, jabbing it at the day's Top Ten Spelling words.

"As we can see," he said solemnly, "there is a nasty ridge of high pressure, followed by several dangerous-looking isobars, just over the English Channel, and these will reach..."

"Wajid Haq!"

Wajid dropped the pointer as Mr Parson's voice rang out.

"Get back to your seat this minute!" he roared. "Otherwise *you* will be experiencing a nasty ridge of high pressure – in the Head Teacher's office!"

Shamefacedly, Wajid replaced the pointer and slipped back into his seat.

"Miss Bannigan will be along – with two very important visitors – in just a few minutes," Mr Parsons told them. "I trust we can rely on Year Five to make as good an impression as possible?"

"Yes, Mr Parsons," chorused Melanie and Jasbir, nodding their heads and glaring at the rest of the class to make sure they joined in.

"I hope so," said Mr Parsons tersely. "Or I can assure you – heads will roll."

And, giving the front two desks a terrible look that left no one in any doubt as to whose heads it would be, he left.

Chapter Three

The classroom door swung open and Miss Bannigan appeared, looking more than usually flushed and excited.

"Welcome to Year Five – my happy band of Eco-Warriors!" she called, ushering in the two very important visitors.

The first was a tall young man with curly pink-tipped blond hair, wearing a tight T-shirt with *Let's Go GREEN!* printed in bright green letters, and a pair of extremely baggy black trousers whose hems polished the floor as he walked. He was followed by a slim young woman with long dark hair in bunches, a green baseball cap and a T-shirt with the same design.

"This is Shazia Khan, and Sean Sting," said Miss Bannigan, looking round Year Five's excited faces. "But I'm sure they need no introduction!"

"Let's go what?" asked Sean, beaming at everyone and giving a thumbs-up sign. They all chorused obediently:

"As you know," Miss Bannigan went on, "Sean and Shazia are going all over the country looking for schools to take part in *Let's Go GREEN!*"

She smiled broadly at Sean, who winked

back. "And, of course, if Grimstone Primary is chosen, one of you will be the Kid Presenter," he added. "Anyone think they're up for it?"

Almost every hand in the class shot up.

"Great!" said Shazia. "What we want are kids who really care about the environment. Kids with oodles of personality..."

"...who can talk about 'green' issues in a really punchy way!" Sean finished.

"You know the kind of thing..." Shazia went over to Miss Bannigan's desk and sat down on a pile of Spelling books. "Litter, pollution, global warming..." she read from the green plastic clipboard on her lap.

There was a sound of chairs scraping at the back of the class and Melanie and Jasbir were on their feet. "Jasbir and me have a great act we've been practising for our Environmental Awareness project!" Melanie said breathlessly. "It's an anti-litter song. We do it like cheerleaders, and we know all the steps. And we've got pom-poms, and whistles..."

She paused for breath and Jasbir took over. "I've got pink sparkly legwarmers and Melanie's got cowboy boots and a white pleated skirt and a real cheerleader's T-shirt with 'Miami Dolphins' on it in pink-and-gold sequins..."

Shazia, who had been scribbling all this information down, looked over at Sean and beamed.

"Just the ticket!" Sean said. "Anyone else?" He looked round, raising his eyebrows encouragingly. A few more hands went up, and Shazia made a note of who they were and what their act was. Wajid sat silently, occasionally giving Wallace a longing look.

"How about you, Wallace and Wajid?" Miss Bannigan said brightly, fluttering her blue eyelids at Sean. "Wallace and Wajid always have such interesting ideas, haven't you, boys?"

Wallace craned round in his seat. Melanie and Jasbir glared at him. He glanced at Wajid and wrinkled his brow. Then, throwing caution to the winds, he began.

"Well, actually, yes – Wajid and me have got all sorts of ideas to make the playground more attractive, and Wajid here's very good at presentation. Got a lovely speaking voice and great delivery, haven't you, Wajid?" he added, smiling proudly at Wajid. "Not to mention several very smart suits."

Wajid blushed, but nodded.

"Wallace, you said your name was?" Sean said, writing it down.

"Wallace Meek." Wallace nodded. "'Meek by name, but not by nature', as my father says. I come up with the ideas and Wajid here presents them. We're a great team."

"Wallace and Wajid..." repeated Shazia. "Sounds kind of cool. So what had you got in mind?"

Wallace looked at Wajid, searching for inspiration, but Wajid looked back blankly. In his mind's eye Wallace could just see Wajid, in his dark blue jacket, sitting behind a desk surrounded by lights and cameramen. He looked wildly around the classroom, searching for an idea.

"We have this plan, to make the playground 'greener'," he said slowly. "And we'd do it as a kind of presentation, with drawings and diagrams and things..."

"And a catchy slogan, of course," put in Wajid.

"So," said Shazia, jumping down from the desk, "you'll be ready to audition tomorrow, will you?"

Wallace and Wajid looked at one another, gulped, and nodded.

"Sure," they said hoarsely. "Course we'll be ready."

Chapter Four

"So what *is* the idea for making the
playground 'greener'?" Wajid asked Wallace.

Wallace shrugged. "What's the catchy
slogan?" he asked in reply, but Wajid
shrugged too.

It was the end of the day, and they were on
their way to Wallace's father's shop, Meek's
Antiques, which, as Wallace had explained to
Wajid to make sure he wasn't disappointed,
was really more of a junk shop than a real
antique shop.

"I've no idea," Wajid admitted apologetically, as Wallace pushed open the shop door. "Just thought it would make a good impression. Television people are really into slogans."

"We need to find a new angle," Wallace sighed. "But nothing to do with litter – that's Melanie and Jasbir's territory and we'd better not tread on their toes." Then he smiled at Wajid. "Welcome to Meek's

Antiques. It's sure to inspire us!"

Meek's Antiques was as full as a shop could possibly be. Ancient chests of drawers heaved under the weight of leatherbound books and old gramophones and china jugs and bowls and plates. Feather boas and hats hung from the ceiling, and garlands of artificial flowers hung in great loops over everything. Wajid gasped. It was certainly inspiring!

From behind a very untidy counter, a rather portly man appeared.

"Hello, Dad," Wallace said, pushing Wajid gently into his father's line of vision. "This is Wajid, and he's come to tea."

"Charmed to meet you, Wajid, and I trust you like broccoli?" Wallace's father smiled and shook Wajid's hand, peering short-sightedly through spectacles that were even thicker than Wallace's.

Wallace motioned to Wajid to follow him, and crawled under a table at the back of the shop. The table was covered with a heavy fringed tablecloth and when you were under it, it felt like being in a tent. When they were both inside, Wallace flicked the switch of a lamp that stood on top of a pile of books, and the tent was bathed in cosy pink light.

"This is my Thinking Spot," Wallace smiled. He switched on a little radio and soft music surrounded them. "Care for a tea biscuit?"

Wallace reached over and lifted an old-fashioned biscuit tin, which he handed to Wajid. On the lid there was a picture of a pretty woman being handed a bunch of red roses by a dashing young man. Underneath was written *Say It With Flowers* in fancy gold letters.

Suddenly Wallace whistled. "This is it, Wajid! The Thinking Spot never fails!"

Wajid looked at Wallace expectantly. "How do you mean, Wallace?" he asked.

But Wallace had crawled out from beneath the table and was deep in conversation with his father.

"I'll be glad to see the back of them, Wallace," his father said, reaching up and detaching a long strand of artificial flowers. "Cheap and nasty, and they catch the dust. If it helps you and Wajid with your project, you're welcome. But do give them a wash."

He filled Wallace's arms till they overflowed, then took three bunches of extremely dusty red plastic roses out of a vase and added them to the pile.

Wajid, his head poking out from under the tablecloth of the Thinking Spot, watched in baffled silence as Wallace collected a roll of paper from behind the counter. Then he moved to one side as Wallace joined him again, dragging with him some of the flowers and the paper.

"What ARE you up to Wallace?" Wajid asked. "How on earth do we get on television with a roll of paper and fifteen metres of dusty flowers?"

"Just you watch, Wajid," said Wallace mysteriously, as he took the lid off a black felt-tip pen. "All will be revealed..."

Chapter Five

The playground was deserted when Wallace and Wajid arrived at school early next morning, and in the silence of S.P.E.W. they unfurled three large rolls of paper and gave their idea one last inspection.

The first two sheets of paper showed aerial views of The School Playground (Before) and The School Playground (After).

On The School Playground (Before) they had taken great care to draw and label every detail, including the bicycle sheds and S.P.E.W. (which they had renamed "Wheeliebin Area" to avoid confusion). It was a very dull and colourless map.

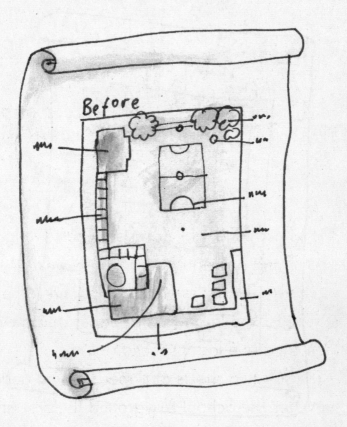

The School Playground (After) was quite a different story. Every available space was filled with carefully drawn trees and grassy patches and, to the left of S.P.E.W., a roughly rectangular area they had labelled New School Garden.

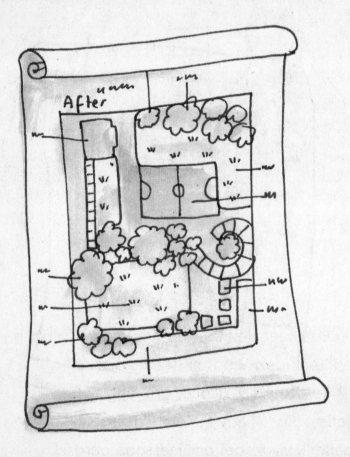

The third piece of paper was the biggest, and by far the most impressive. It had been very difficult to carry, because it was stuck with plastic flowers. They flattened it and held the corners down with their feet and, in silence, surveyed their creation. Then Wajid spoke.

"It's sheer genius," he breathed. "What a brilliant idea, and all from a biscuit tin!"

"Yes," said Wallace, grinning with satisfaction. *Say It With Flowers.* What better way to get our message across!"

The third piece of paper was a detailed plan of the proposed New School Garden. Round the outside they had stuck the heads of about a hundred blue and yellow flowers to form a frame. Then, using the school colours of red and purple, they had spelled out the words: "CARE FOR YOUR EAR".

Wallace frowned down at the garden plan. "Looks a bit silly without the 'TH'," he sighed. "Pity we ran out of red flowers..."

"Don't worry, Wallace," Wajid assured him, waving the bunch of dusty red plastic roses. "We've still got time to use these ones – we'll cut the heads off at lunchtime. I've brought glue and scissors."

There were signs of life coming from the main part of the playground, and they rolled up their visual aids and sauntered casually round to see what was going on.

Melanie and Jasbir had attracted a large circle of onlookers and were practising their cheerleader "litter" song. They held little pom-poms, which they shook as they marched, and chanted:

"Two, four, six, eight
Litter's what we really HATE
Pick it up!
Pick it up!
Ra! Ra! Ra! Ra!"

"CAN'T HEAR YOU!" roared Melanie, waving her arms wildly at the crowd. "Again – louder!"

They repeated their routine as the other children obligingly joined in, and Wallace and Wajid slipped past them into the school. Clutching all their bits and pieces, they ran past the caretaker's room, noting from the sound of the radio that Mr Grubb was already hard at work.

It took them three goes to squeeze the rolls of paper through the classroom door, and when they had managed it they put them carefully under Miss Bannigan's desk and sat down, exhausted.

"Shall we have a listen on the Radio Aid, Wajid?" suggested Wallace. "See whether Miss Bannigan's arrived?"

"Sure," said Wajid, plugging it in. There was a rustling sound, which meant that Miss Bannigan had forgotten to switch the transmitter off again, and they settled themselves comfortably with their heads together to await further developments.

And sure enough, soon they heard a huge whoop of delighted surprise from the teacher.

"Flowers!" she cried, her voice so high it nearly blew their heads off. "For me?"

Then, much fainter and very much less enthusiastic, they heard Mr Parson's voice.

"I believe they're from Mr Sting," he told her. "Red roses, no less. Apparently Mr Grubb's got them in his room."

Wallace looked at Wajid, and Wajid looked at Wallace.

"Romantic, or what!" whispered Wajid. "Isn't that nice?"

"I suppose it is..." said Wallace, a little doubtfully.

"Oh, I think it's wonderful!" Wajid went on. "Sean Sting must be really rich, and you must admit he's very good-looking too. The perfect man for Miss Bannigan."

But Wallace's head was down. Miserably, he drew little circles with his finger on the desktop.

"Next thing will be he'll propose to her and whisk her off to his luxury penthouse flat," he muttered darkly. "She'll be Mrs Sting, Wajid, and that'll be the end of it for us. We'll have to have a new teacher!"

He sat, deep in thought, for a while. Then he sighed deeply.

"I used to think the worst that could happen would be her marrying Mr Parsons," he said, his voice hoarse with gloom. "Now I'm not at all sure..." And with another long sigh, he went back to listening.

But Wajid had jumped to his feet and was looking around in alarm.

"What's wrong, Wajid?" Wallace asked.

"The plastic flowers!" Wajid gasped. "I must've dropped them!"

In the distance they heard the bell ring.

"Come on!" said Wallace, heading out of the classroom. "There's not a second to lose!"

Chapter Six

"And just where do you two think you're going?"

Mr Parsons, buffeted on all sides by children anxious to get to their classes, took hold of Wallace and Wajid's shoulders and swivelled them round to face in the same direction as everyone else.

"We've lost something, Mr Parsons. We have to find it!" Wallace pleaded.

"It's an essential piece of equipment, Mr Parsons," added Wajid.

"I'll 'essential-piece-of-equipment' you," Mr Parsons told them grimly. "If it's so essential you should have looked after it. Now it can wait till break." And he deposited them back outside Year Five's door, where they were met by a very flushed Miss Bannigan.

"I wonder, Mr Parsons," she said breathlessly, "if you would look after my class for just two ticks while I go to Mr Grubb's room and collect my flowers?" And she was gone, before Mr Parsons could decide whether he really wanted to or not.

The classroom was seething with excitement. Melanie and Jasbir had laid out their costumes, and every surface seemed to be covered with pom-poms and batons and white cowboy boots.

"Now, don't forget – join in!" Melanie told everyone, and they all nodded obediently.

"Particularly at the 'Ra! Ra! Ra! Ra!' bit," added Jasbir.

"Give it all you've got," concluded Melanie, using one of Miss Bannigan's favourite phrases.

"Seats, everyone!" Mr Parsons said firmly.
Everyone had just scuttled into place when
the door flew open and Miss Bannigan stood
staring angrily across the classroom. "Mr
Parsons," she said tersely. "May I see you for
a moment?"

And they both disappeared outside and
closed the door.

"Quick!" said Wallace. "Plug it in!"
Everyone gathered round as they adjusted
the Radio Aid. They all looked mystified and
upset.

"Whatever has happened to poor Miss Bannigan?" said Jasbir.

"She was really upset," said Melanie, her bottom lip quivering in sympathy.

"Shhh!" said Wallace. "It's hard to pick her up..."

Wallace and Wajid closed their eyes and concentrated hard. They could only hear odd words here and there but, as it dawned on them what had happened, a look of panic filled their faces.

"How could he...? Just lying on the floor outside Mr Grubb's room... Filthy, plastic flowers... Never been so insulted in my life..."

Mr Parsons' deep voice broke in. "It's preposterous! Wait till I see him! I'll give him a piece of my mind..."

At this, Miss Bannigan's voice rose to a high-pitched squeak. "Oh, Peter," she said, "please don't do anything rash..."

"No – really, Mandy," Mr Parsons' voice was resolute. "You deserve better than that..."

Wallace and Wajid stood up, unplugging themselves as they did.

"There's been a misunderstanding," Wajid muttered. "We'd better go and explain..."

"Must we?" said Wallace, tugging at his sleeve. But Wajid was adamant.

"Of course we must. If Mr Parsons gives Sean a piece of his mind, it'll ruin our chances of getting picked. And anyway, we've got to get our flowers back!"

He led the way to the classroom door, and Wallace trailed reluctantly after him.

Chapter Seven

Wallace and Wajid opened the classroom door a fraction and stuck their heads out. Mr Parsons, who had turned to march off in search of Sean Sting, stopped in his tracks. Miss Bannigan gave a little gasp and let the bunch of dirty plastic roses drop to the floor.

Both teachers stared in horror at the two heads, then Mr Parsons spoke.

"What the devil do you two mean by interrupting us?" he growled. "Can't you see Miss Bannigan and I are having an important meeting?"

"I'm sorry to disturb you, Mr Parsons," Wallace said, "and normally I wouldn't, but Wajid here is feeling rather sick. Probably just nerves, but you never know."

Wajid gazed, speechless, at the teachers and Wallace gave him a dig in the ribs behind the door. There was no reaction, so he put his foot on top of Wajid's and squashed it hard. At last, Wajid got the message and gave a low moan and a couple of coughs.

"Oh Miss Bannigan, I don't feel at all well..." he muttered.

Miss Bannigan put her arm round Wajid. "Oh dear," she said sympathetically, leading him out. "Best take him to the toilet, Wallace..."

When they had disappeared from view, Wallace and Wajid headed straight for Mr Grubb's room. There was a *DO NOT DISTURB* notice on the door and from within could be heard the sound of soft music.

Wallace knocked, and Mr Grubb opened
the door.

"What is it? I'm in the middle of *Desert
Island Discs*," he growled, the unmistakable
scent of roses wafting around him.

"We've come to collect Miss Bannigan's
flowers," said Wajid.

Mr Grubb gave a grunt, went back in, and
returned with an enormous bouquet of red
roses tied with a shiny ribbon. He dumped
the flowers into Wallace and Wajid's arms,
and sneezed.

"Glad to see the back of 'em," he muttered.
"Play havoc with my tubes..."

"Come on, Wajid," Wallace said as they staggered along the corridor under the weight of the flowers. "We've got to get back before Sean Sting arrives."

But as they rounded the last corner, their hearts sank. The classroom door was closed, the plastic roses gone, and bounding towards them was the enthusiastic figure of Sean Sting.

"Wait!" Wallace and Wajid shouted in unison.

Sean, his hand on the door, stopped and turned in amazement to see the walking bunch of roses. "Hey!" he said in a puzzled voice. "Aren't those my flowers? Hasn't Miss Bannigan got them yet?"

Wallace looked at Wajid, and Wajid looked at Wallace. Silently they handed the bouquet over to Sean, and Wajid held the door open for him.

"Nicer to give them to her yourself," he smiled.

"More romantic," muttered Wallace dismally.

There was a great gasp from everyone in Year Five as Sean Sting swept in and, with a flourish, presented Miss Bannigan with the flowers.

"These are from Shazia and myself," he said as he laid them in her arms. "To wish you and Year Five all the luck in the world this afternoon." He turned to the class and gave them a thumbs-up sign.

"Right, folks!" he said. "Let's go what?"

And, deafeningly, they all yelled back,

Miss Bannigan, blushing to the roots of her hair, buried her face in the flowers and breathed their perfume happily.
And in the general chaos, no one noticed Wallace Meek creep over to the wastepaper bin to retrieve his dirty plastic roses.

Chapter Eight

Wajid Haq, his *Let's Go GREEN!* baseball cap perched at a jaunty angle, sank back against the wheeliebins and smiled ecstatically. It was the morning after the auditions, and Wallace and Wajid were still in a happy haze.

"Tell you what, Wallace," Wajid sighed. "That was my finest hour!"

Wallace grinned over at him. "You were brilliant," he said, sincerely.

"Couldn't have done it without you," Wajid replied.

The auditions had gone wonderfully well. Everyone had given it all they had got, and Miss Bannigan had told them they had made her very proud indeed. Melanie and Jasbir's cheerleader routine had been flawless, and everyone had remembered to join in with the "Ra! Ra! Ra! Ra!"s.

But the "Playground Improvement Presentation" had been the star act. Wallace and Wajid had drafted in all the children who were too shy to perform themselves, and got them to hold up both The School Playground (Before) and The School Playground (After) diagrams. Then Wajid had used the blackboard pointer to explain everything in a voice which Miss Bannigan had later described as "clear as a bell".

Wallace had remained in the background, waving his arms about a lot and generally directing operations.

Everything had gone like a dream, but it was the New School Garden idea that had clinched it.

"That is *it*!" Sean had said, rapturously, as the "CARE FOR YOUR EARTH" design wobbled and then came to rest in front of his eyes. "It'll make perfect television. We'll film you all digging and planting, and we'll have 'before' and 'after' shots, and then we'll add music and speed it all up so the viewers see the garden appear before their eyes!"

"And we'll have Melanie and Jasbir and all the others dancing round it..." added Shazia dreamily, "...in green, billowy costumes..."

"And of course," added Sean, *Let's Go GREEN!* will supply everything. Grimstone Primary will get a complete makeover!"

Then the moment of truth had arrived. They had all gone back into the classroom, and Shazia had stood in front of them with her clipboard, waiting to announce who was to be Kid Presenter.

"My heart was in my mouth," Wajid told Wallace for the fourth time. "I was sure she was going to pick Melanie or Jasbir. You've got to admit – they were very slick!"

Wallace nodded. "They were. But we were slicker!"

Wajid hugged his knees. "We're going to be Kid Presenters, Wallace! Can you believe it? My television career has begun!"

And they gave each other a thumbs-up sign and sighed happily.

"There's just one fly in the ointment, Wajid," Wallace said quietly, suddenly looking very serious. "I'm still worried about Miss Bannigan and Sean Sting. Even if the flowers weren't meant to be romantic, he does like her, you can tell. And he's going to be around for weeks making the programme, so he'll have loads of chances to win her over..."

But Wajid shook his head.

"Don't you worry, Wallace," he told him. "I heard something yesterday afternoon, after you'd gone home..."

Wallace sat up and looked at Wajid's Radio Aid.

"You haven't been withholding information?" he asked, frowning.

"Of a very sensitive nature!" Wajid tapped the side of his nose and smiled knowingly. "Wanted to choose my moment, if you know what I mean..."

The bell rang and Wajid stood up. "Let's just say there's nothing like a bit of healthy competition," he added, "to hurry things along. We're in for a bit of a surprise, Wallace."

And they certainly were. From the very moment Miss Bannigan stepped into the classroom, everyone knew there was something different about her.

It wasn't just that her cheeks were pinker, and her eyes more brightly glowing, than ever before. It wasn't just that her smile was more dazzling than it had ever been. And, when she told them to sit on the floor round her seat because she had something Very Special to tell them, it wasn't just that her voice was softer and sweeter than they had ever heard it.

Melanie and Jasbir spotted it first. They clung together for a moment, and then they whispered to everyone around them and told them to "pass it on".

And when the message reached Wallace, and he saw what it meant, he bit his lip so hard it almost bled, as he dug his fingernails deep into Wajid's sleeve.

"It's OK," whispered Wajid, patting Wallace's hand comfortingly. "Remember what I told you ... healthy competition!"

"Year Five," Miss Bannigan said softly, holding up her left hand so they could all see the diamond ring that sparkled from her fourth finger, "I am engaged to be married to..."

She paused. Wallace edged forwards and gazed up, waiting with bated breath.

"Mr Parsons," Miss Bannigan smiled down at them.

"Oh, miss!" everyone breathed. "Congratulations!"

They all pushed forward to get a better look at the engagement ring, and Wallace and Wajid drifted away.

"Ah well, Wajid – it could be worse," said Wallace philosophically. "At least Mr Parsons won't whisk her away to a luxury penthouse flat..."

"He's not that bad, deep down," said Wajid generously. Then he smiled broadly, pointed to the Radio Aid, and winked.

"And he can be ever so romantic when he puts his mind to it!"

Young Hippo
**Terrific stories, brilliant characters
and fantastic pictures – try one today!**

There are loads of fun books to choose from:

Jan Dean

Alan MacDonald

Penny Dolan

Mary Hooper

Frank Rodgers

Franzeska G. Ewart

Margaret Ryan